Picasso
at the Lapin Agile

by

STEVE MARTIN

A SAMUEL FRENCH ACTING EDITION

SAMUEL
FRENCH
FOUNDED 1830

New York Hollywood London Toronto

SAMUELFRENCH.COM

ISBN 978-0-573-69564-3   Printed in U.S.A.   #18962

THE PROMENADE THEATRE

Under the Direction of Ben Sprecher and William P. Miller

Opening: October 22, 1995

STEPHEN EICH   JOAN STEIN
LEAVITT/FOX THEATRICALS/MAGES

Present

Picasso
at the Lapin Agile

A New Play by
STEVE MARTIN

Starring

CARL DON   SUSAN FLOYD

HARRY GROENER   TIM HOPPER

PETER JACOBSON   JOHN CHRISTOPHER JONES

GABRIEL MACHT   MARK NELSON   RONDI REED

Scenic Design	Costume Design	Lighting Design
SCOTT BRADLEY	PATRICIA ZIPPRODT	KEVIN RIGDON

Sound Design	Wigs and Hair
RICHARD WOODBURY	DAVID H. LAWRENCE

General Manager	Production Stage Manager
ALBERT POLAND	MARK COLE

Associate Producters
JERRY C. BRADSHAW   GEORGE A. SCHAPIRO/YENTL PRODUCTIONS

Directed by
RANDALL ARNEY

Originally produced at STEPPENWOLF THEATRE CO., Chicago, October, 1993
RANDALL ARNEY, Artistic Director   STEPHEN EICH, Managing Director

PICASSO AT THE LAPIN AGILE

*A bar in Paris, 1904. One year later, Albert Einstein
published the Special Theory of Relativity.
Three years later, Pablo Picasso painted
"Les Demoiselles D'Avignon."*

by **Steve Martin**

Cast in Order of Appearance:
Freddy, the owner and bartender of the Lapin Agile
Gaston, an older man
Germaine, waitress and Freddy's girlfriend
Albert Einstein, age twenty-five
Suzanne, age nineteen
Sagot, Picasso's art dealer
Pablo Picasso, age twenty-three
Charles Dabernow Schmendiman, a young man
The Countess
A female admirer
A visitor

PICASSO AT THE LAPIN AGILE

(A bar in Paris, The Lapin Agile, circa 1904. A bartender, FREDDY, rubs a rag across the bar. On the wall is a three by four foot painting of some sheep in a landscape. Upstage left is a door from the street. Upstage right is a door to a hall and toilet. We hear prerecorded accordion music of "Ta rah rah Boom dee ay". FREDDY the bartender is taking chairs off the tables.)

GASTON. *(Offstage. Singing.)* Ta rah rah Boom dee ay, Ta rah rah Boom dee ay, Tah rah rah Boom dee ay, Tah rah rah Boom de ay.

(A man about sixty, GASTON, enters.)

GASTON. *(Singing.)* Ta rah rah Boom dee ay, Ta rah rah Boom dee ay, Ta rah rah Boom dee ay, Ta rah rah Boom dee ay.

FREDDY. Well, Gaston, you sound like you're out of your bad mood.

GASTON. Yes, dammit. Woke up this morning, good mood. Nothing I could do about it. Ta rah rah Boom de ay, Ta rah rah Boom de ay... Damn my memory, what's the next lyric?

FREDDY. I don't know, but my guess is it's Ta rah rah Boom dee ay.

GASTON. Great song. I wonder who wrote it?

FREDDY. Two East Indian guys. Ta Rah and Rah Boom Dee ay.

GASTON. *(Sits, then.)* I have to pee.

FREDDY. Already? You haven't had a drink yet.

GASTON. One day you'll understand.

(GASTON gets up, moves toward the toilet. Through the door, EINSTEIN, age 25, enters, hair slicked and neat looking.)

EINSTEIN. I'll be sitting there. I'm to meet a woman.

GASTON. *(To EINSTEIN.)* Oh shut your face you little pipsqueak!

FREDDY. *(To GASTON.)* Hey! You don't even know him.

GASTON. I have a feeling.

FREDDY. Still, you can't just insult someone right out of the blue.

GASTON. But I'm French.

(GASTON exits.)

EINSTEIN. Do you have absinthe?

FREDDY. One absinthe coming up.

EINSTEIN. I'm supposed to meet her at six o'clock at the Bar Rouge.

FREDDY. This is not the Bar Rouge. It's the Lapin Agile.

EINSTEIN. No difference.

FREDDY. No difference?

EINSTEIN. You see, I'm a theorist and the way I see it is that there is just as much chance of her wandering in here accidentally as there is of her wandering into the Bar Rouge on purpose. So where I wait for her is of no importance. It is of no importance where I tell her I will be. And the least of all, it's not important what time I am to meet her.

FREDDY. Unless...

EINSTEIN. Unless what?

FREDDY. Unless you really want to meet her.

EINSTEIN. I don't follow.

FREDDY. If you really want to meet her, you'll go to the Bar Rouge at the time you told her.

EINSTEIN. You're forgetting one thing.

FREDDY. What's that?

EINSTEIN. She thinks like I do.

FREDDY. Here's your vodka.

EINSTEIN. I asked for absinthe.

FREDDY. No difference.

(EINSTEIN takes the drink and sits down. GASTON re-enters.)

GASTON. I can describe the woman you're waiting for.

EINSTEIN. So can I!

GASTON. But I've never seen her. I can describe her hair, her clothes, her smell even.

EINSTEIN. Go ahead.

GASTON. But I need something.

EINSTEIN. Like what?

GASTON. Women are my area of expertise. And, like the paleontologist, I can reconstruct the creature from a bone. But, I need a hint.

EINSTEIN. How did you get to be such an expert?

GASTON. By looking.

EINSTEIN. So you're an admirer of the feminine equation?

GASTON. Yes, but I never touch. It's my saving grace. In that way I glide among them, invisible. So I need a hint.

EINSTEIN. Yes, a hint. She has long red hair.

GASTON. Ah. One of those. Hard to control because she's so damn pert. She runs you, doesn't she? Her speech will be short, like her skirt. She'll sit over there and cross her legs and control the room. She's controlling it now. Look at us, talking about her all because she has long red hair.

EINSTEIN. Sounds like you really know women.

GASTON. Never met one really.

EINSTEIN. Never met one?

GASTON. Not in my new incarnation as an older man. Women respond differently to men of different ages. I'm only newly old. Just getting used to it really. My name is Gaston.

EINSTEIN. My name is Albert Einstein.

(FREDDY looks up suddenly.)

FREDDY. You can't be. You just can't be.

(FREDDY crosses from behind the bar and approaches EINSTEIN.)

EINSTEIN. Sorry, I'm not myself today. *(He fluffs his hair, making himself look like EINSTEIN.)* Better?

FREDDY. No, no, that's not what I mean. In order of appearance.

EINSTEIN. Come again?

FREDDY. In order of appearance. You're not third. *(Takes playbill from audience member.)* You're fourth. It says so right here. Cast in order of appearance. I knew you were fourth. I knew it when you walked in.

EINSTEIN. And yet you said nothing?

FREDDY. I couldn't put my finger on it. But now I can. *(Gives back the program.)*

EINSTEIN. I take your point. Toilets!

GASTON. Behind that door.
EINSTEIN. Thank you.

(EINSTEIN exits. The waitress, GERMAINE, thirty-five, enters. She is FREDDY'S girlfriend.)

GERMAINE. Sorry I'm late.
GASTON. You're not late, you're third.

(GERMAINE walks behind the bar, pours herself a drink and swallows it.)

FREDDY. Where were you?
GERMAINE. At home, darling.
FREDDY. Doing what?
GERMAINE. Sitting in front of a mirror.
FREDDY. Why?
GERMAINE. Just looking. Seeing what all the fuss is about. Besides, a mirror is like a mind, if you don't use it, it loses the power to reflect.
FREDDY. Well you should try and be on time, sweetheart.
GERMAINE. Oh, don't be so old fashioned--these are the naughts.
FREDDY. This is the fourth day you're late.
GERMAINE. Are we going to fight? Let's not fight, Freddy. Let's be in love like yesterday. *(She kisses him.)* So tomorrow I can say, "Let's be in love like yesterday." *(She kisses him again.)* Always. *(Another kiss.)* Always.
FREDDY. *(Breaks away.)* Okay, always.
GERMAINE. *(Walks away.)* I love you, even though you give me nothing.

FREDDY. What?
GERMAINE. *(As in "oh nothing".)* Nothing.

(EINSTEIN re-enters, again from the street. He perfunctorily goes through his dialogue, panting.)

EINSTEIN. I'll be sitting there. I am here to meet some-one. A woman. I am to meet her at six o'clock. At the Bar Rouge. *(Then, to FREDDY.)* All right?
GERMAINE. Bar Rouge? This is not the...
GASTON and EINSTEIN. Don't ask.
GERMAINE. Hey, Gaston. See any good ones today?
GASTON. Saw a good one yesterday as the shops were closing. I tried to hold her in my memory but she faded. All I remember now is a white linen blouse with just a whisper of brassiere underneath. It was like seeing a sweet custard through a veil of meringue.

(An attractive nineteen-year-old girl, SUZANNE, comes through the door. She is street smart and in charge, and there's probably a few more broken hearts just from her walk to the Lapin Agile.)

SUZANNE. I've heard Picasso comes here. *(Pause. They all look at her.)* Does he?
FREDDY. Sometimes.
SUZANNE. Tonight?
FREDDY. Maybe.

(This pleases SUZANNE. She takes an article of clothing out of her bag. She turns her back to the audience and unbut-

tons her blouse, but before she takes it off, she stops and speaks first to FREDDY.)

SUZANNE. Look away. *(Then to EINSTEIN.)* You look away too. *(Then she looks at GASTON.) I guess you're okay. (She takes off her blouse, revealing a black bra underneath, and puts on a new, sexier top.)* Okay.

(They ALL turn. SUZANNE sits at a table and waits.)

GASTON. *(After a pause.)* Damn!
FREDDY. What's the matter?
GASTON. Now I have to consider everything I'm wearing today to be lucky. Every time I go out now, it's "not without my lucky hat, not without my lucky coat, not without my lucky shirt."
SUZANNE. I'd like some wine.
GERMAINE. Any special color?
SUZANNE. Red please.

(GERMAINE gets the wine from FREDDY.)

GERMAINE. Do you know Picasso?
SUZANNE. Twice.
GERMAINE. Is he expecting you?
SUZANNE. *("Of course")* I think he's expecting to see me.
EINSTEIN. Who is this Picasso?
GERMAINE and FREDDY and SUZANNE. *(Simultaneously.)* He's a painter...
FREDDY. He's a painter, or says he's one. I've never seen his paintings, only what he says. Nuts about blue, they say.
SUZANNE. Oh, yes. He's a painter. I've seen them. He gave

me a drawing.

FREDDY. What are they like?

SUZANNE. They're strange, really. Not like that, I'll tell you.

(SUZANNE refers to the sheep painting on the wall.)

FREDDY. Nothing wrong with this picture. Got it out of my grandmother's house just after she died; well, actually while she was dying. Sheep in a meadow in the fog. Beautiful.

EINSTEIN. That's not what I see.

FREDDY. And what do you see, *Einstein?*

(The "Einstein" has a pejorative emphasis.)

EINSTEIN. I prefer to take it further. Observe how the sheep are painted small, consumed by the weather and the terrain. So I see "the power of the landscape over the small things." For me, it's the meaning that gives it its value.

GASTON. *(Dismissive.)* Jesus Christ! Sheep. Meadow. Fog. Period.

GERMAINE. There's a problem.

EINSTEIN. What?

GERMAINE. Well, it seems to me, if you judge it only by its meaning, then any bad painting is just as good as any good painting if they have the same meaning.

(There is a long, long pause while everyone thinks.)

EINSTEIN. Women!

GASTON. I would like a wine. The purpose of the wine is to get me drunk. A bad wine will get me as drunk as a good wine. I would like the good wine. And since the result is the same no matter which wine I drink, I'd like to pay the bad wine price. Is that where you're headed, Einstein?

FREDDY. I really don't think he's that clever, Gaston.

SUZANNE. *(She reaches in her bag and produces a folded up piece of paper.)* Want to see the drawing he gave me?

(SUZANNE hands it to EINSTEIN. He gets up, walks downstage holding the drawing up and examines it in the light.)

EINSTEIN. I never thought the 20th century would be handed to me so casually... scratched out in pencil on a piece of paper. Tools thousands of years old, waiting for someone to move them in just this way. I'm lucky tonight; I was open to receive it. Another night and I might have dismissed it with a joke, or a cruel remark. Why didn't it happen before, by accident? Why didn't Raphael doodle this absentmindedly?

FREDDY. What do you think of the drawing?

EINSTEIN. *(Innocent.)* What could it matter?

FREDDY. Huh? Let me see it. *(He looks at it.)* Hmmm. Yeah.

GERMAINE. *(She looks at it.)* I like it all right.

GASTON. I don't get it.

SUZANNE. I don't think it looks like me.

EINSTEIN. There you go. Four more opinions. I wonder how many opinions the world can hold. A billion? A trillion? Well, we've just added four. But look, the drawing stays the same.

FREDDY. *(He takes EINSTEIN'S glass to fill it.)* Hey look. What kind of a person would I be if I didn't form an opinion? I see the drawing, I think about it, I form an opinion. Then I see other people and I express my opinion. Suddenly, I'm fascinating. *(He drinks EINSTEIN'S drink.)* And because I'm so fascinating, someone else sees the drawing, and they have an opinion and they're fascinating too. Soon, whereas before I was standing in a room of dullards, I am now standing in a room of completely fascinating people with opinions.

SUZANNE. My name's Suzanne.

GASTON. And you're waiting for Picasso.

SUZANNE. Right. Do you know him?

GASTON. I've heard of him a bit. Big guy, rodeo rider, trick roper?

SUZANNE. Uh, no...

GASTON. What's his first name?

SUZANNE. Pablo.

GASTON. Oh, no. Different guy. So how did you meet Pablo?

SUZANNE. I... it was about two weeks ago. I was walking down the street one afternoon and I turned up the stairs into my flat and I looked back and he was there framed in the doorway looking up at me. I couldn't see his face because the light came in from behind him and he was in shadow and he said "I am Picasso." And I said, "Well so what?" And then he said he wasn't sure yet but he thinks that it means something in the future to be Picasso. He said that occasionally there is a Picasso and he happens to be him. He said the twentieth century has to start somewhere and why not now. Then he said, "May I approach you?" and I said okay. He walked upstairs and picked up my wrist and turned it over and took his fingernail and scratched deeply on the back of my hand. In a second, in red, the image of a dove appeared. Then I thought, why is it that someone who wants me can hang around for months, and I even like him but I'm not going to sleep with him, but someone else says the right thing and I'm on my back, not knowing what hit me.

GERMAINE. Yeah, why is that?

FREDDY. Huh?

GERMAINE. Never mind.

SUZANNE. See, men are always talking about their things. Like it's not them.

GASTON. What things?

SUZANNE. The things between their legs.

GASTON. Ah, yes. Louie.

FREDDY and EINSTEIN. Ah...

SUZANNE. See! It's not them; it's someone else. And it's true; it's like some rudderless firework snaking across town. But women have things too, they just work differently. They work from up here *(She taps her head.)*. So when the guy comes on to me through up here, he's practically there already, done. So the next thing I know he's inside the apartment and I said, "What do you want?" and he said he wanted my hair, he wanted my neck, my knees, my feet. He wanted his eyes on my eyes, his chest on my chest. He wanted the chairs in the room, the notepaper on the table; he wanted the paint from the walls. He wanted to consume me until there was nothing left. He said he wanted deliverance, and that I would be his savior. And he was speaking Spanish, which didn't hurt, I'll tell you. Well at that point, the word "no" became like a Polish village. *(They look at her, waiting, then.)* Unpronounceable. *(Proud.)* I held out for seconds. Frankly I didn't enjoy it that much 'cause it was kinda quick.

GASTON. Premature ejaculation?

GERMAINE. Is there any other kind?

FREDDY. Huh?

GERMAINE. Never mind.

SUZANNE. So then, as I was sitting there half dressed, he picked up a drinking glass, of which I have two, and looked at me through the bottom. *(She picks up a glass and demonstrates.)* He kept pointing it at me and turning it in his hand like a kaleidoscope. And he said, "Even though you're refracted, you're still you." I didn't ask. Then he said he had to be somewhere and I thought, "Sure," and he left.

GERMAINE. You saw him again?

SUZANNE. Oh yeah. That night he comes back with this drawing and gives it to me, and we do it again. This time in French. I enjoyed it this time if you're keeping score. Then he gets very distracted and I said, "What's the matter?" and he said he sometimes starts thinking about something and can't stop. Wait, he said he doesn't think about it, he sees it. And I said, "What is it?" and he said, "It can't be named." Well, when you're with someone who says they're seeing things that can't be named, you either want to run like hell or go with it. Well, I'm going with it and that's why I'm here tonight. He told me about this place, that he might see me here one day, and that was two weeks ago.

GASTON. Sex, sex, sex.

SUZANNE. What?

GASTON. Oh nothing, I was just thinking out loud.

SUZANNE. Been awhile?

GASTON. About eight months. Interesting really. I saw a cat in the street and bent over to pet it and it moved just out of my reach. It seemed friendly but nervous so I followed it, always moving out of my reach. It must have been two feet out of my reach for several blocks, here kitty, kitty, kitty, when I realized the cat had stopped at the feet of a woman. I looked up at her and our eyes met. Older, my age, but she was dazzling. Let's just say she had a nice mortal coil. We made love in her place within the hour.

SUZANNE. Did you ever make love to her again?

GASTON. No, I didn't.

SUZANNE. See, there you are. She was there; you were taken with each other. You men. Why is once enough? Why wouldn't you make love with her again?

GASTON. I would have but she died about an hour later.

SUZANNE. Oh.

GASTON. We both wanted to do it again and I told her I needed an hour to rejuvenate. I went outside and sat with the cat and after a while I looked up and they were taking her body out on a stretcher.

SUZANNE. Oh my God.

GASTON. I can't help but think that I killed her.

(Pause, then GASTON emits a low, prideful chuckle.)

FREDDY. What did Picasso say about my place?

(FREDDY starts sifting through some bills.)

SUZANNE. He said this is where artists come to talk about... let's see... mana... mana...

EINSTEIN. Festos? Manifestos?

GERMAINE. Anyone want a coffee?

GASTON. *(Vehement.)* That's what I could go for!

GERMAINE. Cream or black?

GASTON. No, a manifesto! I could really go for a nice juicy manifesto. It would be nice to wake up and have a *raison d'etre* to go with your morning coffee, wouldn't you say? I have to pee.

(GASTON exits to the loo.)

EINSTEIN. Did Picasso say he was working on a manifesto?

SUZANNE. Oh no. He said he doesn't need one and if he did come up with one he would have exhausted it before he finished writing it down. Oh, one other thing. Just before he left he went to the window and reached down on the sill and like lightning, grabbed a pigeon. Then he held it in one hand and turned it upside down and he soothed it and talked to it and it was like the pigeon fell asleep. Like it was hypnotized. Then he held his hand out the window and dropped the pigeon. And it just fell two stories upside down, straight down, like a stone. Then just seconds before it would have hit the ground, the pigeon turned itself over and started flapping like mad and it took off flying, straight up past us, above the buildings and just away into the night. Then Picasso turned to me and said, "That's like me." And he was gone. Could I have a refill?

(GASTON re-enters.)

GERMAINE. I'll get it. Anyone else want a refill?

(Several respond.)

FREDDY. Anybody know what 62 francs 33 minus 37 francs 17 is?

GERMAINE. Why don't you let me do that, Freddy?

EINSTEIN. 25 francs 16.

FREDDY. You sure?

EINSTEIN. 25.16.

FREDDY. You're positive.

EINSTEIN. Positive. Absolutely.

FREDDY. It's just that you came up with it awfully quick.

EINSTEIN. Look, if you want it to be different there's nothing I can do about it.

FREDDY. I'll work on it tomorrow.

EINSTEIN. It'll be the same tomorrow.

FREDDY. I've got my accountant friend coming over tomorrow; he can check it. He checks everything anyway.

EINSTEIN. You can have a math squad from the Vishnu Numerical Center For The Intellectually Profound come over and it's still going to be 25 francs 16.

FREDDY. All right, all right.

GERMAINE. Jeez, Freddy. Take his word for it.

FREDDY. Are you a professor?

EINSTEIN. No, I'm not.

FREDDY. What do you do?

EINSTEIN. By day I work in the patent office.

GERMAINE. What do you do there?

EINSTEIN. By day I register notions. That's what they are really, notions. Short cuts. How to get something to do something quicker.

GERMAINE. And what do you do at night?

EINSTEIN. Ah. At night... at night, the stars come out.

GERMAINE. The stars in the sky?

EINSTEIN. The stars in my head.

GERMAINE. And after the stars in your head come out?

EINSTEIN. I write it down.

FREDDY. Uh huh. You been published?

EINSTEIN. No, no not yet.

FREDDY. Yeah, well, we're all writers, aren't we? He's a writer that hasn't been published and I'm a writer who hasn't written anything.

(FREDDY goes back to his bills.)

GERMAINE. And you're welcome here. We get a lot of artist types; writers, poets, painters. What do you write about?

EINSTEIN. I... I... I can't even begin to explain.

GERMAINE. Try. Simplify it. Can you say what it's about in one sentence?

EINSTEIN. It's about everything.

GERMAINE. You mean like relationships between men and women?

EINSTEIN. Bigger.

GERMAINE. You mean like life from birth to death?

EINSTEIN. Uh, bigger.

GERMAINE. Like the warring of nations and the movements of people?

EINSTEIN. Bigger.

GERMAINE. I see, sort of like the earth and its place in the solar system?

EINSTEIN. Keep going.

GERMAINE. *(Growing exasperation.)* Okay. You're dealing with the universe and everything contained in it.

EINSTEIN. Why stop there?

GERMAINE. *(Giving up.)* Okay. Okay. How big is this book?

EINSTEIN. About 70 pages.

GERMAINE. Hmmm, not too long. That's good. Maybe we can put you in contact with some of our publisher friends. What's the title?

EINSTEIN. The Special Theory of Relativity.

FREDDY. *(Sincere.)* Catchy.

GASTON. Judging from the title alone, I think it will sell at least as well as the Critique of Pure Reason.

GERMAINE. Is it funny?

EINSTEIN. *(Thinks.)* Well...

GERMAINE. Because if it's funny, you can really sell a lot of books.

EINSTEIN. It's very funny.

GERMAINE. Ah! It's very funny.

EINSTEIN. Well, actually, that depends on what you mean by funny.

GERMAINE. Well, does it make you laugh?

EINSTEIN. No.

GERMAINE. Chuckle?

EINSTEIN. No.

GERMAINE. Smile?

EINSTEIN. I wish I could say yes.

GERMAINE. So it's not funny.

EINSTEIN. No.

GERMAINE. But you just said it was funny.

EINSTEIN. I was trying to sell more books.

GERMAINE. *(Exasperated.)* Could it have illustrations?

EINSTEIN. Impossible.

GERMAINE. Why not? Might look good, give it some zip.

EINSTEIN. Illustrations are two-dimensional.

GERMAINE. I know what you mean, but a good draftsman can give very realistic three-dimensional drawings.

EINSTEIN. I need four.

GERMAINE. Einstein, I'm trying to help you here. You want your book to have impact, don't you?

EINSTEIN. Sure.

GERMAINE. And if you want it to have impact you've got to have people read it, don't you?

EINSTEIN. Yes...

GERMAINE. Okay, in your field, how many people do you figure have to read your book to have some impact?

EINSTEIN. One.

GERMAINE. No, no, no. In order for your book to have impact, you've got to have a lot of people read it; every man in the street has got to have one.

EINSTEIN. No, only one. Max.

GERMAINE. Max?

EINSTEIN. Max Planck, a German physicist, very influential. If he reads it, he makes my reputation.

GERMAINE. Well, you're lucky. If your market is one person and you know his name, you can put a limit on what you're going to spend on advertising. How old are you?

EINSTEIN. I'm 25.

GASTON. You don't look 25.

EINSTEIN. I discovered at an early age that I am the kind of person who will always look 86.

FREDDY. Hey Einstein, last week I bought twelve bottles of Chablis at 17 francs a bottle but only eleven came. How much do I owe this guy?

GERMAINE. Leave him alone.

EINSTEIN. 187 francs.

FREDDY. See? As long as we've got him here we might as well use him. I made a deal with Alphonse for a case of port at 26 francs each. He said if I bought six cases he'd give me a discount of two to four percent. But he didn't know the year of the port. He said, if the port arrived and was newer than 1900, he'd give me a four percent discount, keeping three percent on bottles before 1900 and two percent on bottles before 1895. When I got the cases, two cases had nine bottles dated after 1900 and fifteen bottles dated before 1895. One case had eighteen percent of the bottles dated before 1900 and the rest were evenly split between before 1895 and after 1900. The rest of the three cases after 1900, before 1900 and before 1895 respectively. How much the hell do I owe this guy?

GERMAINE. Oh good grief!

FREDDY. Oh, I left out one thing. He said if the sum total of the digits of the date of a bottle was greater than 25 he would give a nine percent discount on those bottles.

EINSTEIN. Hmm.

FREDDY. He's stumped.

EINSTEIN. Oh sorry, I wasn't listening. HA! Just kidding. Here's your answer: 2245 francs 73 given that x end parenthesis y is the mean price per bottle.

FREDDY. 2245. Did you say y end parenthesis x?

EINSTEIN. Y end parenthesis x? *(Laughs heartily.)* OH... THAT'S FUNNY!

(EINSTEIN continues laughing, pretty soon, they're all laughing but they're not sure why.)

FREDDY. What's the date today?

GERMAINE. It's the eighth.

FREDDY. And the year?

GERMAINE. You don't know the year?

FREDDY. I know the year... it's just that sometimes when you're writing fast it's easy to write down the wrong year. Sometimes I look at a date I've written and it's off by ten, sometimes fifteen years. But now that I'm thinking about it I know it's 1903.

GERMAINE. '04.

FREDDY. *(Quickly.)* '04. Okay... come on, the year just changed. It's only January.

GERMAINE. October.

FREDDY. The date isn't important anyway.

EINSTEIN. Just put, "first decade of the twentieth century."

GERMAINE. Gosh, that's what it is, isn't it? The first decade of the twentieth century. I'm glad the nineteenth century is over. It was a bad century.

FREDDY. What's there not to like about a century?

GERMAINE. Well, for one thing, the pollution. Soot, garbage, smoke.

GASTON. Horseshit.

GERMAINE. You disagree?

GASTON. No, I'm adding to the list.

GERMAINE. Oh yeah... *(Continuing.)* Horse shit. Noise.

EINSTEIN. This century will be better.

FREDDY. What do you see for the future?

EINSTEIN. Let me ask you. What do you see?

GERMAINE. I'll answer. I see air travel becoming common, with hundreds of people being carried in giant "airplanes." I think we'll see images sent through the air and the receivers will become so popular that mass taste will diminish their potential. The city of Hiroshima will be completely modernized. *(EINSTEIN'S head jerks toward her.)* There will be a brief craze for lawn flamingos. Vast quantities of information will be stored in very small spaces. Cruelty will be perfected. By the end of the century, smoking in restaurants will be banned.

GASTON. Oh brother.

FREDDY. Uh huh.

SUZANNE. *(Dismissive.)* Right.

EINSTEIN. *(Yeah sure.)* Next.

GERMAINE. Oh well fine.

FREDDY. Here's mine. Led by Germany, this will be known as the century of peace. Clothes will be made of wax. There will be a craze for automobiles but it will pass. The French will be the military might of Europe. Everyone will be doing a new dance called the "toad." A carton of cigarettes will be one of the most thoughtful get-well gifts. And the Wright brothers will be long remembered for the invention and manufacture of a low-calorie fudge.

(Everyone nods, "Sounds about right... could be," etc. A man enters, early fifties and a bit rotund, nattily dressed. It is SAGOT, vibrant and energetic. He goes over to FREDDY.)

SAGOT. Anyone in tonight?

FREDDY. Not that you're looking for, Sagot.

SAGOT. I got a Matisse today, small but juicy. A little beach-scape... give me a rum... I got him to give it to me. Here take a look. *(He pulls out a small 4"x5" canvas and hands it to FREDDY.)* It says everything about Matisse you want to know. I bought eight drawings and got him to throw it in. The smaller it is, the harder it is to say it, no doubt about it, and that thing's got it all. Stick it up there, Freddy. *(He indicates the bar. FREDDY hands him a drink and puts the painting up on the back bar. SAGOT stands back.)* Look at it... Beautiful. *(He moves back a few more feet, stops.)* ... Still works... *(A few more feet, stops.)* ... Still working. Still holds the wall. *(He moves as far back as he can, stops.)* Lost it there. But damn, you see what I mean?

SUZANNE. Not really.

SAGOT. Up to ten feet away, that bar is working for the Matisse. Then the bar takes over. *(He downs the rest of the drink.)* One more, Freddy.

GASTON. Does anyone feel a draft in here?

EINSTEIN. *(Indicates the Matisse.)* What makes it so great?

SAGOT. You want to know what makes it so great? I'll show you what makes it great. *(He goes to the bar and picks up the Matisse. He takes it out of its frame. He hold up the frame.)* This is what makes it great.

GASTON. The frame?

SAGOT. The boundaries. The edge. Otherwise anything goes. You want to see a soccer game where the players can run up into the stands with the ball and order a beer? No. They've got to stay within the boundaries to make it interesting. In the right hands, this little space is as fertile as Eden.

EINSTEIN. That frame is about the size of my book.

SAGOT. Well I hope you chose your words carefully. Ideas are like children, you have to watch over them or they might go wrong.

FREDDY. I know what he means.

SAGOT. *(To EINSTEIN.)* I told that to Apollinaire; he squiggled and squirmed. *(To the Matisse.)* I'm going to turn a nice profit on that, you watch.

FREDDY. Well, considering you got it for free, it might not be too difficult.

EINSTEIN. But you got it because you loved it. How can you sell it?

SAGOT. What do you do?

EINSTEIN. I'm a physicist.

SAGOT. Good. Then you must know how naive a question can sound. I'll tell you how it works. *(SAGOT is drinking all the time through this.)* When I bought it, I identified it. I identified it as something worth having. I have named it as a work of art. Once I've done that, I don't have to own it. It will always be mine. And I guarantee you Matisse is happy about it too. He wants his work out there, out of Paris. I've sold to Russia and I've sold to America and I've sold to dealers in Paris who've sold everywhere. And the dealers like to buy from me because frankly they don't get it, and they want me to discern the good ones from the bad ones.

EINSTEIN. How did you learn to tell the difference?

SAGOT. I wish I knew! But I can look at two pictures that no one has ever seen before and know that one is for me *(He points in the air.)* and that one *(He points to a different place.)* is for the people whose idea of art is something ugly done by a relative. They come to the galleries with bags of money and say, "Show me what you've got, taste is no object!" *(He finishes drink.)* Another, Freddy.

FREDDY. Finally a customer.

SAGOT. Freddy, take out the book.

FREDDY. Come on...

SAGOT. No, take it out. *(FREDDY takes out a large book with engraved art plates. He opens the pages. SAGOT looks at the engravings only.)* Courbet!... *(Another page.)* Courbet! *(Another page.)* Courbet!

FREDDY. Wait a minute, this is a book about Courbet.

(FREDDY gets another book, opens the page and shows it to SAGOT.)

SAGOT. Titian! *(SAGOT takes a drink. FREDDY thumbs through the book and moves to a different plate.)* Raphael! *(SAGOT takes a drink; FREDDY shows another plate.)* Hmm that's a tough one.

GASTON. You got the other ones, what's so tough about that one?

SAGOT. He's got his thumb over the name. *(He laughs big at his joke.)* We art dealers are notorious for our sense of humor!

FREDDY. All right. All right. That's enough. *(SUZANNE hold up the PICASSO drawing and challenges SAGOT. He turns and sees it. SAGOT smiles.)*

SUZANNE. Who's this?

(SAGOT takes the drawing.)

SAGOT. Was he here this evening?
GERMAINE. Not yet.
SAGOT. Are you meeting him here?
SUZANNE. Don't know.
SAGOT. I can wait. *(He looks more closely at the drawing.)* A trifle hasty. Do you want to sell it?
SUZANNE. Not for anything.
SAGOT. For fifty francs?
SUZANNE. It is mine *forever.*
SAGOT. *(Giving up.)* Get him to sign it. It'll be worth more.

(SAGOT sits down.)

GERMAINE. *(Indicates the painting on the wall.)* Hey

Sagot, you're the expert, what do *you* see?

SAGOT. *(Takes a short look.)* Oh that. I see a five hundred pound lemon.

FREDDY. What?

GASTON. I have to pee.

(GASTON exits.)

SAGOT. I know that there are two subjects in paintings that no one will buy. One is Jesus, and the other is sheep. Love him as much as they want, no one really wants a painting of Jesus in the living room. You're having a few people over, having a few drinks, and there's Jesus over the sofa. Somehow it doesn't work. And not in the bedroom either, obviously. I mean you want Jesus watching over you but not while you're in the missionary position. You could put him in the kitchen, maybe, but then that's sort of insulting to Jesus. Jesus, ham sandwich, Jesus, ham sandwich; I wouldn't like it and neither would He. Can't sell a male nude either, unless they're messengers. Why a messenger would want to be nude I don't know. You'd think they'd at least need a little pouch or something. In fact, if a nude man showed up at my door and I asked, "Who is it?" and he said, "Messenger," I would damn well look and see if he has a pouch and if he doesn't, I'm not answering the door. Sheep are the same, don't ask me why, can't sell 'em.

(SAGOT sits down.)

GASTON. *(Re-entering.)* Here's what I don't get. A month goes by, every night no different than tonight. People come in, people go out. So why do all the nuts show up in one evening?

GERMAINE. Picasso's definitely coming in tonight.

SUZANNE. I hope he comes in.

FREDDY. Me too. He owes me a bar bill.

EINSTEIN. I'd like to meet him.

SAGOT. Maybe I could get a painting out of him.

GERMAINE. Well, we all have an interest in Picasso; let's give a little toast to him.

EINSTEIN. I'll do it... To ... Pi...

(They all raise their glasses. Through the door, Picasso enters, age 23. A little like Rodin's sculpture of Balzac *only quicker. Moody, brooding.)*

PICASSO. I have been thinking about sex all day. Can't get it out of my mind.

GASTON. I've been thinking about it for 62 years.

PICASSO. I did 16 drawings today, 2 in pencil, the rest in ink. All women. What does *that* tell you? It tells me a painter has got to stay well-fucked, otherwise the mind drifts off the easel, out the window and across the street to the grocer's daughter. *(To EINSTEIN.)* You were proposing a toast.

EINSTEIN. Oh yes, to... Picasso.

PICASSO. Hey, To him. I mean did you talk about anything else besides me? Did the weather come up?

EINSTEIN. It was mostly about you.

PICASSO. God, I feel good! How lucky for you! To be talking about someone and then in they come. Anyway, how do I look, be honest. That spot! *(He points to the sheep painting.)* We've got to do something about it. *(To SAGOT.)* Why don't you come by tomorrow? I have something to show you. Something's afoot. The moment is coming; I can feel it.

SAGOT. The last month's work has been spectacular. I sat in front of the last piece I got from you with some friends and explained it for two hours.

PICASSO. Did they get it?

SAGOT. Don't know. They left after the first hour. I can tell you that the last hour was lonely hard work.

PICASSO. Forget it. That was piss, piss I tell you. This is different already. There is nothing in my way anymore. If I can think it I can draw it. I used to have an idea, then a month later I would draw it. The idea was a month ahead of its execution. Now, the idea is ahead of the pencil only by minutes. One day, they will be simultaneous. *(He stands up, to the room.)* Do you know what that's like? If you can think it you can draw it? The feeling of clear undiluted vision?

EINSTEIN. *I* have a vague idea.

PICASSO. Are you an artist?

EINSTEIN. No, I'm a scientist, but sometimes I feel like an artist.

PICASSO. *(Jazzy.)* Well, multiply it by a thousand and you know what it's like to be me. *(He notices SUZANNE, scrapes his foot on the floor like a bull.)* I don't believe we've had the pleasure.

SUZANNE. Well, *you* have.

PICASSO. My name's Picasso.

SUZANNE. How nice for you.

PICASSO. *(He picks up her hand, scratches on the back of it with his nail. She doesn't look at it.)* Look at it.

SUZANNE. It's a dove. *(She takes out her drawing and walks over to SAGOT.)* How much?

SAGOT. Fifty francs. *(To PICASSO.)* That's a good price isn't it?

PICASSO. *(Realizing.)* Yes, that's fair.
SUZANNE. It's the price of fame I guess.

(SUZANNE starts to leave, but stops on PICASSO'S next line.)

PICASSO. *(He gets up and walks over to SAGOT.)* How much for the drawing?
SAGOT. Whatever you want.
PICASSO. *(He reaches in his pocket for money but he has none. He finds a pencil and sketches some lines on a napkin, finishes and hands it to SAGOT.)* Fair?
SAGOT. Very fair; this one's signed.

(PICASSO takes the original drawing and kneels before SUZANNE, offering it to her. She accepts it; he starts to go.)

SUZANNE. Sign it. *(SAGOT silently claps. PICASSO signs it.)* I would like another drink.

(SUZANNE sits.)

PICASSO. *(To the room.)* And I would like... a motorcar! Can I do that, Sagot? Can I draw my way into a car? Can I draw a camera and you sell it and suddenly I can have a camera? Can I get anything I want by just drawing it?
GERMAINE. *(To SAGOT.)* Can he?
SAGOT. Not yet.
PICASSO. And don't worry because I never would. And don't forget it.
SAGOT. Anyway, if you need a camera, I've got one.

PICASSO. Good. Wait a minute. You have a camera?

SAGOT. Yes. I have a camera.

PICASSO. How did you get the camera?

SAGOT. I bought it.

PICASSO. Well I have one question. If I can't afford a camera, how can you afford a camera? How much are you selling my paintings for?

SAGOT. Twice what I pay for them.

PICASSO. TWICE? Twice! I'm so depressed.

FREDDY. Actually that's not so bad. You should hear what I'm making on the drinks.

PICASSO. Now there's *two* words I can't stand: "twice" and "perky." *(Suddenly.)* God he's good. I hate him! *(He crouches, tightening his body and grimacing.)* I hate him! I... hate... *(He straightens his body, turns and points to the Matisse on the bar.)* HIM! Just when you're in the swing of things, someone has to come along and ruin it for you. *(He picks it up, looks at it.)* It's so NEW. I can't even be mad. This is not painting, it's alchemy! Ouch! It's sizzling hot! *(He sets down the Matisse.)* Take it from me, folks, the boy can paint. What's he like?

SAGOT. What's he like? He's earnest, talented obviously, nice to be around...

PICASSO. Ugh.

SAGOT. ... self-deprecating...

PICASSO. Good. It saves me the trouble. *(He parks himself against the bar, turns to the others, and grins. Then suddenly, looking at the sheep painting on the wall.)* See Sagot, here's the difference between you and me. You look at that nasty old thing and see a picture of some sheep in a landscape.

GASTON. He's not the only one.

PICASSO. Right! He's not the only one. Enter... me! I see it differently. I see it as an empty frame with something hideous in it that's waiting to be filled up with something NEW. *(He picks up a pencil and hold it like a foil.)* Advancing out into the unknown, the undrawn, the new thing must be coaxed out of its cave, wrestled with and finally pinned up on the wall like a hide. When I look at Goya, it's like he is reaching his hand through the centuries to tap me on the shoulder. When I paint, I feel like I am reaching my hand forward hundreds of years to touch someone too.

GASTON. So it's like a relay.

(PICASSO goes over to SUZANNE, picks her up and starts dancing with her, no music, she's reluctant at first. They dance for a while.)

EINSTEIN. I work the same way. *I* make beautiful things with a pencil.

PICASSO. You? You're just a scientist! For me, the shortest distance between two points is *not* a straight line!

EINSTEIN. Likewise.

PICASSO. *(Still dancing.)* Let's see one of your creations. *(EINSTEIN pulls out a pencil. PICASSO stops dancing, gets a pencil. The others back away like it's a western shootout.)* Draw!

(PICASSO and EINSTEIN start to draw on the table tops. EINSTEIN finishes first.)

EINSTEIN. Done! *(They swap drawings.)* It's perfect.
PICASSO. Thank you.

EINSTEIN. I'm talking about mine.

PICASSO. *(He studies it.)* It's a formula.

EINSTEIN. So's yours.

PICASSO. It was a little hastily drawn... Yours is letters.

EINSTEIN. Yours is lines.

PICASSO. My lines mean something.

EINSTEIN. So do mine.

PICASSO. Mine is beautiful.

EINSTEIN. *(Indicates his own drawing.)* Men have swooned on seeing that.

PICASSO. Mine touches the heart.

EINSTEIN. Mine touches the head.

PICASSO. *(Holds his drawing.)* Mine will change the future.

EINSTEIN. *(Holds his drawing.)* Oh, and mine won't?

(Sensing victory, or at least parity, EINSTEIN starts to dance with SUZANNE. PICASSO stands befuddled.)

PICASSO. Maybe you're a fake.

EINSTEIN. And maybe you're an *idiot savant.* And hold the *savant.*

(EINSTEIN continues dancing, the old man watches.)

GASTON. *(Suddenly singing.)* WHEN A MAN LOVES A WOMAN...

(GASTON stops.)

FREDDY. What the hell was that?

GASTON. I don't know, it just came over me.

(SAGOT gets out of his chair and starts to exit.)

FREDDY. Where're ya going?

SAGOT. I'm going to get my camera. A night like this must be preserved on film. *(Referring to the painting on the wall.)* Picasso, do something about that ovine pastorale, will you?

PICASSO. The idea is coming.

SAGOT. I like it; sounds good.

(SAGOT exits.)

PICASSO. The idea is coming. THE idea is coming.

(EINSTEIN dances SUZANNE to her seat. He signs his drawing and gives it to her.)

FREDDY. Hey, tell me if you get this joke. A man goes into a bakery and says "Can you mail a pie?" The baker says, yeah I think we could. Then the man says, "Well could you bake me a pie in the shape of the letter E?" And the baker says, "Yeah I think we could do that. Come back tomorrow and we'll have it for you." So the man comes back the next day and the baker shows him the pie. The man says, "You idiot! That's a big E. I wanted a small E, a small E." So the baker says, "No problem, come back tomorrow and I'll see what I can do." So the man comes back the next day and the baker shows him the pie. The man says, "Perfect... it's perfect." Then the baker says, "So where do you want me to send it?" And the man says, "You know what... I think I'll eat it here." *(They all stare at him. No laughs.)* Guy told me that the other day; I didn't get it.

GERMAINE. It's surreal.

FREDDY. I guess that's why I didn't get it. I'm a symbolist.

GERMAINE. And a good for nothing one at that.

FREDDY. You calling me a good for nothing symbolist?

SUZANNE. What's symbolism?

GERMAINE. So far it's an excuse for not doing the dishes.

FREDDY. That's not fair. Your post-romanticism has gotten us into a lot of hot water around here.

GERMAINE. My romanticism is not *post*!

FREDDY. It most certainly is!

GERMAINE. It's *neo.*

FREDDY. Post!

GERMAINE. Neo!

FREDDY. Post!

GASTON. STOP IT BOTH OF YOU! My God! This is not some sleazy dive somewhere.

EINSTEIN. The reason the joke is funny is the perfect selection of the letter E. It couldn't be a A-shaped pie, because A is functioning as both article and noun; who needs it? It can't be a B-shaped pie because of the confusion of the letter B with the insect. And not a C-shaped pie either, because that customer never would have known that it was a capital C pie, since C looks the same in both upper case and lower case pie. *(Thinks.)* I'll come back to D. An F-shaped pie is just plain not funny. An H-shaped pie would be unstable: two vertical bars supported by a weaker crossing structure. An I-shaped pie is not good because of the dot problem: do you connect the dot to the pie, in which case it's not really an i; or do you keep it separate, which raises the question, is it a dot or is it a cupcake?

A K-shaped pie has Kafka written all over it. An M-shaped pie doesn't work because of the M-W dilemma: M to whom? And need I mention sigma? An O-shaped pie doesn't work because a pie *is* O shaped. A P-shaped pie doesn't work because the phrase "P-shaped pie" has this naughty calypso rhythm!

GASTON. Excuse me, you're not going to go through the entire alphabet, are you? Because I may only have a few good years left.

EINSTEIN. Of course not, some of them are so obvious they needn't be mentioned. Like Q for example.

(Big pause while everyone thinks.)

GERMAINE. All right, what's the matter with Q?

EINSTEIN. Well a Q is just an O with a comma through it, and a comma shaped pie is just a croissant.

GERMAINE. Thank you.

SUZANNE. You said you would come back to D.

GASTON. NO! I have to L... I mean pee.

(GASTON exits to the bathroom.)

FREDDY. Wait a minute, you said the joke was funny. But it wasn't funny.

EINSTEIN. Oh yes it was. *I* laughed.

GERMAINE. No you didn't

EINSTEIN. Not now, no. I'll laugh later. An ice box laugh.

FREDDY. An ice box laugh?

EINSTEIN. Yes. You don't laugh now, but an hour later you're at home, standing in front of the ice box and you laugh.

GASTON. *(Offstage.)* E-shaped pie! Hahahahahaha.

EINSTEIN. See? He's just getting it now. Probably through a process of elimination. [*Author will be in the downstairs lobby when this joke is delivered*] *(To FREDDY.)* When did you hear the joke?

FREDDY. A year and a half ago.

EINSTEIN. Maybe you already laughed at that joke but thought you were laughing at something else.

FREDDY. You mean, something else funny happened, and I laughed but really I was laughing at this joke, which I may have heard a year ago?

EINSTEIN. Right.

FREDDY. So I might still "owe" a laugh at the other funny thing that happened?

EINSTEIN. Or not. You may have only thought the other thing that happened was funny, but it really wasn't so you don't owe a laugh.

FREDDY. So instead of laughing at the thing I thought was funny, I was laughing at the thing I didn't think was funny.

EINSTEIN. Exactly.

FREDDY. There's only one problem.

EINSTEIN. What?

FREDDY. The thing that you think that I think wasn't really funny was when the cat went running across the kitchen floor to leap through the cat door but it was locked. Now there's no way that wasn't funny.

PICASSO. How about you, my dear? What do you say?

SUZANNE. I've had my example of a bad joke.

PICASSO. *(Sits.)* Oh come on.

SUZANNE. You're a womanizing bastard fraud.

PICASSO. If you're trying to praise me that's a poor choice of words.

SUZANNE. You're ridiculous.

PICASSO. Look, I meant everything I said that night, I just forgot who I said it to. Stranger things will happen in your young life, believe me. Worse things.

SUZANNE. I believed you.

PICASSO. I believed it too. And now that I see you tonight, my dear, I'm believing it all over again. I remember a blue-green bed with a rose colored spread over it. A tin half-moon on the wall, holding a candle. On your bedside table there were three rings side by side with small turquoise stones, one with garnet, and next to them a pale pink ribbon. Later I picked it up off the floor. I can't remember your name.

SUZANNE. I never told it to you.

PICASSO. Yes, you did. I remember it now.

SUZANNE. I never told you.

PICASSO Yes you did Suzanne.

SUZANNE. I don't remember.

PICASSO. My ear was inches from your mouth. You said your name to me, then spoke words half-whispered, words started and left unfinished, mixed with cries, passion obscuring their meaning. *(He leans in and kisses her.)* Do you remember?

SUZANNE. Yes.

PICASSO. I drew three pictures of you from memory.

SUZANNE. You did?

PICASSO. But I can do better.

SUZANNE. I'll be there later.

PICASSO. That's a coincidence. So will I.

SUZANNE. I should go now. *(She picks up her things.)* Good-bye everyone. *(She goes over to EINSTEIN.)* Good-bye, Al. *(To PICASSO.)* When will you be there?

PICASSO. When the play's over.

(SUZANNE exits.)

EINSTEIN. *(Laughing.)* The cat door was locked!

(GASTON re-enters from the bathroom.)

GASTON. So who's the third?

FREDDY. What do you mean?

GASTON. Well in this bar tonight are two men; one is Einstein, the other Picasso, both nearly the same age, who think that somehow their work is going to change the century. So let's give it to them and say they are. One. Two. There must be a third; there's always a triptych, the father, the son and the holy ghost, the three graces, not to mention that bad news always comes in threes. Need I say more?

EINSTEIN. So who is the third point in the triangle, so to speak?

GERMAINE. Maybe it's Matisse.

PICASSO. No! Matisse cannot be third! If he wants he can be fourth or fifth, but he cannot be the third point in the triangle.

EINSTEIN. I hate to tell you this but the idea of a triangle with four points will not fly. A triangle with four points is what Euclid rides into hell.

GERMAINE. Well, who is the third?

(Enter SCHMENDIMAN, bursting in.)

SCHMENDIMAN. You are lucky tonight. You were here

at the moment and you heard it straight from the horse's mouth. I will be changing the century. The other bars know it, you may as well too.

EINSTEIN. And what is your name?

SCHMENDIMAN. Schmendiman. Charles Dabernow Schmendiman.

EINSTEIN. And how will you change the century?

SCHMENDIMAN. With my invention.

PICASSO. What is your invention?

SCHMENDIMAN. It's an inflexible and very brittle building material.

EINSTEIN. Oh? What's it made from?

SCHMENDIMAN. And I'll tell you what it's made from: equal parts of asbestos, kitten paws, and radium. The only problem with it is that building considerations only allow it to be used in Los Angeles, San Francisco, and the island of Krakatoa, East of Java. But still! That's a big market! So everyone have a drink...!

FREDDY. On you?

SCHMENDIMAN. Uh... no. Just have a drink! And remember my name: Schmendiman. *(They ALL say "Schmendiman" rather lamely.)* You see there's a distinction between talent and genius. And it's not just that they are spelled completely different. Talent is the ability to say things well, but genius is the ability to well, say things! Talent sells a million in a year, but genius sells 5000 a year for 200 years! *(To EINSTEIN.)* Can you compute that, or am I movin' too fast for you? You have to work to have talent. But genius comes gift wrapped in a blue box from Tiffany's!

GASTON. Picasso, Einstein and Schmendiman. Somehow it doesn't have a ring.

SCHMENDIMAN. Which one's Picasso? *(GASTON points.)* I've heard of you... nice work. If you like blue. Come to think of it, it's about time for a Spaniard again... I mean, it's been a long time since "Bell-ath-kweth." I'm just needlin' ye! You would be interested in my process. Creation is easy! Just follow the path of least resistance. You're supposed to paint butcha feel like dancin'? DANCE! You're supposed to write butcha feel like singin'? SING! That's what I did. Remember, the shortest distance between two points is a foot and a half. No pun intended.

FREDDY. No pun achieved.

SCHMENDIMAN. I struggled to be a writer but my heart told me to invent a very brittle and inflexible building material, which by the way is called "Schmendimite." And I did! That's why I know my place in history is secure... I followed my heart. Next bar! *(Goes to the door, saying like a cheer:)* Schmenda... Schmenda... Men Men Men! *(He goes out the door, stops suddenly in the doorway.)* Wait! I just had another idea! A tall pointy cap for dunces!

(SCHMENDIMAN snaps his fingers. He exits.)

GASTON. What the hell was that?

FREDDY. I admire his confidence. And nothing else.

EINSTEIN. Here's the way I look at it. We're not so much going to change the century, as bend it. Let's say Picasso here is a genius. The century is just flying along in space and it whizzes by Picasso here and it picks up speed and it flings itself off in a new direction. Like a comet veering left at the sun. The century is just zigzagging along, bending and curving, influenced by the powerful gravity of people like Picasso. But the century itself, because we're in it, appears to be heading straight.

GASTON. How can something be curved but appear to be straight? Come on, buddy.

EINSTEIN. *(Sarcastic.)* Gee, I never though of that. I guess you're right. HOW ABOUT THE HORIZON YOU NITWIT?

GASTON. Are you trying to get my goat?

EINSTEIN. No, I'm just trying to explain something. You'll be happy to know that not only is the horizon something that appears to be straight but is actually curved, but so is space in general.

GASTON. Horseshit.

EINSTEIN. Well it just so happens that it is!

GASTON. Is not!

EINSTEIN. Is too!

GASTON. Is not!

EINSTEIN. Is too!

GASTON. Is not!

GERMAINE. *(To FREDDY.)* Neo.

FREDDY. Post!

GERMAINE. Neo!

FREDDY. Post!

PICASSO. Mine is not a formula!

EINSTEIN. *(To PICASSO.)* Is so!

FREDDY. *(To EINSTEIN.)* Is not!

EINSTEIN. Is so!

PICASSO. *(To FREDDY.)* Neo!

FREDDY. Post!

PICASSO. Neo.

EINSTEIN. Hold it! Not only is space curved but light has mass and it bends when it passes by large masses like the sun at its finite speed of one hundred eighty-six thousand miles per second! *(He gasps.)* Uh oh! *(To everyone.)* Oh my God, I can't believe I just blurted out the ending of my book. What I just said is my business and I hope it won't leave this room.

FREDDY. I'm glad you stopped me; I was just going to the phone.

GERMAINE. You want to hear a woman's opinion on this?

EINSTEIN. There is no woman's opinion. This is science.

GERMAINE. Are you saying women can't be scientists?

EINSTEIN. No! I'm saying there are no gender-related opinions on this matter. Madam Curie didn't say, "I think I've discovered radium, I better check with a man." No man's opinion, no woman's opinion. It's sexless.

GASTON. I know the feeling.

EINSTEIN. What I just said is the fundamental, end-all, final, not-subject-to-opinion, absolute truth depending on where you're standing.

(EINSTEIN sits, exhausted. There is silence in the room. Then...)

PICASSO. Are you through?

EINSTEIN. I am.

PICASSO. So much thinking.

EINSTEIN. You should try it sometime.

GASTON. *(To PICASSO.)* How do you draw something? It seems so impossible.

PICASSO. *(Flip.)* It's all in the wrist.

EINSTEIN. *(He points to his brain.)* And I maintain that the wrist starts here!

FREDDY. I know what he means.

(FREDDY splashes together a drink.)

PICASSO. I put the pencil to the paper and it comes out! Not the craft, mind you, that was difficult to get. The ideas are a different matter. The ideas swoop down on me, they fall like rain, they land with a crash.

EINSTEIN. They "thunk" too.

PICASSO. Absolutely! They thunk.

EINSTEIN. You too?

PICASSO. Yes. And pop.

EINSTEIN. Well, pop all the time, that goes without saying. They never seem to flow though.

PICASSO. Never. Flowing is a myth.

EINSTEIN. Never flow. Well sometimes.

PICASSO. Yeah, sometimes.

FREDDY. Where do they come from?

PICASSO. Before me artists used to get ideas from the past. But as of this moment they are coming from the future, fast and loose.

EINSTEIN. Absolutely from the future.

PICASSO. I think in the moment of pencil to paper the future is mapped out in the face of the person drawn. Imagine that the pencil is pushed hard enough, and the lead goes through the paper into another dimension.

(PICASSO and EINSTEIN start to get excited.)

EINSTEIN. Yes!

PICASSO. A kind of fourth dimension if that's what you want to call it...

EINSTEIN. I can't believe you're saying this! A fourth dimension!

PICASSO. ... and that fourth dimension is... the future.

EINSTEIN. Wrong.

PICASSO. *(Arguing.)* The pencil pokes into the future and sucks up ideas and transfers them to the paper for Christ's sake. And what the hell do you know about it anyway... you're a scientist! You just want theories...

EINSTEIN. Yes, and like you, the theories must be beautiful. You know why the sun doesn't revolve around the earth? Because the idea is not beautiful enough. If you're trying to prove that the sun revolves around the earth, in order to make the theory fit the facts, you have to have the planets moving backwards, and the sun doing loop-the-loops. Too ugly. Way ugly.

PICASSO. So you're saying you bring a beautiful idea into being?

EINSTEIN. Yes. We create a system and see if the facts can fit it..

PICASSO. So you're not just describing the world as it is?

EINSTEIN. No! We are creating a new way of looking at the world!

PICASSO. So you're saying you dream the impossible and put it into effect?

EINSTEIN. Exactly.

PICASSO. Brother!

EINSTEIN. Brother!

(PICASSO and EINSTEIN hug.)

GERMAINE. Oh please. You two are spouting a lot of bullshit and I say the only reason you got into physics and art in the first place is to meet girls.

PICASSO and EINSTEIN. What!!!

EINSTEIN. You actually think I said to myself, "How can I meet a lot of girls; I know, I'll develop a unified field theory?"

GERMAINE. Look, I'm not saying you're not sincere, but let's face it, *(To EINSTEIN.)* you've got some splashy party talk and *(To PICASSO.)* you've got the perfect and oldest pick-up line: I'd like to draw you.

PICASSO. That's outrageous.

GERMAINE. Maybe it's unconscious. I just think that somewhere way back you realized you weren't maybe the hand-somest things around and decided to go a different route.

EINSTEIN. I'm disgusted!

(A woman enters, glasses, brainy, well-dressed, long red hair.)

EINSTEIN. Countess!

COUNTESS. Albert!

EINSTEIN. Did you go to the Bar Rouge?

COUNTESS. Of course not, that's where you said we'd meet.

EINSTEIN. Oh how stupid of me, of course you'd come here.

COUNTESS. Now what was that you were saying about it being impossible to distinguish motion produced by an outside gravitational force?

EINSTEIN. *(Aside.)* God she's sexy!... *(They start to leave, EINSTEIN mumbles.)* It's impossible to distinguish, you know, two bodies unified... in a field...

(The COUNTESS pays. EINSTEIN is a little embarrassed, but not enough to stop her.)

EINSTEIN. *(He turns to the room, suddenly waxing rhapsodic.)* Although we may never meet again, like the roots of the Sequoia grabbing deep in the earth, the ideas we have said here tonight will lace themselves irrevocably through the century.

PICASSO. *(Full of himself.)* This is the night the earth fell quiet and listened to a conversation!

EINSTEIN. *(The same.)* O Lapin Agile!

PICASSO. Picasso, Einstein, Picasso, Einstein. My only regret is that we'll be in different volumes in the encyclopedia.

EINSTEIN. But there'll be no Schmendiman to come between us.

(EINSTEIN exits.)

PICASSO. I envy him.

FREDDY. Why's that?

PICASSO. In science, there's no reason to ever get cynical.

FREDDY. Why would an artist get cynical?

PICASSO. I think it's called marketing.

FREDDY. I've got to run next door and catch Antoine before he leaves town without paying his bar tab. *(To audience.)* I might be gone a longer amount of time than you'd think it would take a person to run next door and catch Antoine before he leaves town without paying his bar tab, but traditionally it's okay.

(FREDDY exits.)

PICASSO. Gaston, don't you have to pee?

*(GASTON realizes he does and exits. PICASSO walks over to
GERMAINE and they kiss... you can tell it's not the first
time. They break.)*

PICASSO. Tasty. Quite tasty.

GERMAINE. What was I? Dessert?

PICASSO. What do you mean?

GERMAINE. I mean how many meals have you had today?

PICASSO. Why be nasty? We're not so different...

GERMAINE. Oh yes, we slept together but there's a difference. Women are your world. For me, you are the thing
that never happened. You and Freddy exist in separate uni-
verses. What I do in one has nothing to do with the other.

PICASSO. How convenient.

GERMAINE. Oh, don't get me wrong. I'm not being nasty.
I like you. It's just that I know about men like you.

PICASSO. Men like me? Where are there men like me?

GERMAINE. Have a drink. You don't want me to go on.

PICASSO. No, tell me about men like me.

GERMAINE. *(Settles in.)* A steady woman is important to
you because then you know for sure you have someone to go
home to in case you can't find someone else. You notice every
woman, don't you?

PICASSO. *(Pause.)* Many.

GERMAINE. I mean every woman. Waitresses, wives,
weavers, laundresses, ushers, actresses, women in wheelchairs.
You notice them, don't you?

PICASSO. Yes.

GERMAINE. And when you see a woman you think, "I
wonder what she would be like." You could be bouncing your

baby on your knee and if a woman walks by you wonder what she would be like.

PICASSO. Go on.

GERMAINE. You have two in one night when the lies work out, and you feel it's your right. The rules don't apply to you, because the rules were made up by women, and they have to be if there's going to be any society at all. You cancel one when someone better comes along. They find you funny, bohemian, irresistible. You like them young because you can bamboozle them and they think you're great. You want them when *you* want them, never when they want you. Afterwards you can't wait to leave, or if you're unlucky enough to have her at your place you can't wait for *her* to leave because the truth is we don't exist afterwards, and all conversation becomes meaningless because it's not going to get you anywhere because it already got you there. You're unreachable. Your whole act is a camouflage. But you are lucky, because you have a true talent that you are too wise to abuse. And because of that you will always be desirable. So when you wear out one woman, there will be another who wants to taste it, who wants to be next to someone like you. So you'll never have to earn a woman and you'll never appreciate one.

PICASSO. But I appreciate women: I draw them, don't I?

GERMAINE. Well, that's because we're so goddamn beautiful isn't it?

PICASSO. Germaine, men want, and women are wanted. That's the way it is and that's the way it will always be.

GERMAINE. That may be true, but why be greedy? By the way, I knew you were using me, but I was using you back.

PICASSO. How?

GERMAINE. Now I know what a painter is like, tomorrow night a street paver maybe, or a news agent, or maybe a bookseller. A street paver may not have anything to talk about to a girl like me, but I can write my romantic scenarios in my head and pull them down like a screen in front of me to project my fantasies onto. Like you project your fantasies onto a piece of paper.

PICASSO. How does Freddy fit in? Why are you with him?

GERMAINE. *His* faults I can live with. And occasionally, occasionally, he says something so stunning I'm just glad to have been there. But really? What I wouldn't give for a country boy.

(FREDDY re-enters.)

FREDDY. Well, I caught the son-of-a-bitch in time.

GERMAINE. Not quite.

(A young woman charges into the bar. She looks around.)

WOMAN. I heard that he comes here. Is that true? I mean is that really true? *(She notices PICASSO.)* OH MY GOD! Oh my God. You. May I approach? May I really approach? *(She walks toward him.)* I can't believe it. What is it like to be you? I mean what is it really like?... *(Looking into his face, her demeanor changes.)* Wait a minute, you're not Schmendiman!

(The WOMAN, bored, walks toward the door, exits.)

PICASSO. Well, another typical night.

(PICASSO wanders over and stands staring at the painting, he becomes lost in it. GASTON re-enters.)

GASTON. I learned something here tonight.

FREDDY. What's that?

GASTON. You take a couple of geniuses, put them in a room together and... wow.

FREDDY. Boy, you really know how to turn a phrase.

GASTON. What I mean is, these two guys are smart. That must be what it takes to be a genius: brains. An incredible amount of brains.

(Enter from the toilet door, A SINGER FROM THE FIFTIES, age twenty-five. He wears blue suede shoes and has jet black hair. Possibly, a guitar is over his shoulder. He dusts himself off, looks around curiously. Some of the dust is stardust. Everyone eyes him as he goes up to the bar, looks at the Matisse painting, wanders away, swivels his hips at GASTON, finds that funny, sits down.)

GASTON. Don't tell me you're a genius too.

SINGER. Shucks no.

GERMAINE. Something to drink?

SINGER. Sorry ma'am, don't drink. Do you have a tomato juice? I'm just a country boy.

(GERMAINE collapses, then gets up.)

FREDDY. Sure we do. You want something in that?

SINGER. Like what?

FREDDY. Well, like vodka.

SINGER. *(Giggles.)* You're kiddin'. *(GERMAINE goes weak in the knees again, gets up.)* By the way, watch the shoes.

FREDDY. What brings you here?

SINGER. Well, I kinda like surprising people, you know, poppin' up where you're least expected, supermarkets, fairgrounds; one thing I like to do is get in people's snapshots so when they develop 'em I'm in their picture. But I got a little bored so I thought I'd do a little time travelin'. Try another time zone.

GASTON. Put some vodka in it.

(The SINGER looks around at the group in the bar.)

SINGER. You seem like some pretty nice folks.

FREDDY. *(Offended.)* Pretty nice folks? What the hell are pretty nice folks?

GERMAINE. Yeah. What are you talking about?

SINGER. Well, you know, friendly, good natured. Accepting of strangers.

FREDDY. Why would I want to be that?

GASTON. Yeah, what the hell are you trying to imply?

SINGER. Well, where I come from that's what people are like.

GERMAINE. Where are you from?

SINGER. Memphis.

FREDDY. Memphis, Egypt?

SINGER. No, sir. Memphis is in America.

("Oh." Silence. FREDDY starts polishing the bar. GERMAINE starts cleaning glasses. GASTON takes a long swig.)

GASTON. What's Hiawatha really like?

(EINSTEIN enters with COUNTESS, tipsy.)

EINSTEIN. *(Talking to countess.)* ... Aparently the cat door was locked. *(He notices where he is.)* Oh my God. We've ended up where we started from.
COUNTESS. *(Nudges EINSTEIN.)* Not only is space curved, so is Paris!

(COUNTESS laughs.)

EINSTEIN. *(To SINGER.)* I don't believe we've met.
SINGER. Oh yes we will.
EINSTEIN. You and I think alike.

(EINSTEIN starts to move toward the SINGER.)

SINGER. Watch the shoes.
EINSTEIN. *(Halts.)* What do you do?
SINGER. Well, ah guess ah... *(Thinks.)* sing songs about love.

(Everybody takes a breath. GERMAINE especially.)

FREDDY. *(Rhapsodic.)* If only I could sing songs about love.
GERMAINE. If I could sing songs about love, I would sing, and remember lovers past, and the emotion would infuse itself into the lyric.
PICASSO. I would give it all up if I could sing songs about

love. No more paints or brushes... just the Moonlight, the Junelight, and You.

GASTON. In the summer evenings I would stand along the Seine and just sing, sing, sing.

EINSTEIN. People crowding in a smoky cabaret to hear the song stylings of Albert Einstein... appearing nightly with the Kentuckymen. Singing songs as pretty as a summer dress... lover's hand going into lover's hand.

SINGER. See what I mean about you all being pretty nice folks?

(They are all embarrassed. SAGOT enters. He is carrying a tripod camera.)

SAGOT. Good. You're all still here.

PICASSO. That's the camera?

SAGOT. The latest.

PICASSO. They're making them so small! Where did you get it?

SAGOT. I bought it from a Japanese tourist. Okay, everybody group together over there.

(They ALL start to primp.)

EINSTEIN. I'd like to order three one by twos and a daguerreotype.

SAGOT. Come everybody. In a row and squeeze together.

(They ALL assemble for the photo.)

GERMAINE. I hate having my picture taken.

SAGOT. *(To the SINGER who hangs out away from camera.)* You get in there too.

SINGER. Oh don't worry. I'll be in it.

SAGOT. Who are you, by the way?

(SAGOT buries his head under the camera cloth.)

SINGER. I guess you could say I'm a messenger.

(SAGOT emerges from under the camera cloth and eyes him up and down, then recovers.)

SAGOT. *(Announcement.)* On this day in 1904, the Lapin Agile was the site of this historic photo.

(SCHMENDIMAN enters.)

SCHMENDIMAN. Did someone say historic photo? *(Takes out compact, powders nose and kneels in front with his arms outstretched.)* Can you still see the others?

SAGOT. Sure can.

SCHMENDIMAN. *(Disappointed.)* Oh.

SAGOT. Okay everybody, smile.

(Erratic smiling. Some do, some don't. It goes in and out. As some get the smile, others lose it.)

SAGOT. Hold it. You're not all smiling.

EVERYBODY. *(Ad lib.)* Well it's difficult, it feels fake Why?... etc.

SAGOT. Okay. Okay. How about this. We'll think up a word that makes the face go naturally into a smile and we'll all say it at the same time.

EVERYBODY. *(Ad lib.)* Yeah, okay... good idea.

(They ALL think.)

SAGOT. Hmm. What's the word.. what's the word. I've got it. Matisse. *(He says it a couple of times to check and his mouth goes into a smile. Everyone tries as they reform in a group. SAGOT gets behind the camera.)* Okay everyone, say "Matisse". One, two, three.

(ALL say it and smile. Except PICASSO who frowns.)

SAGOT. Try again, one more time. Picasso, you're not smiling!

PICASSO. Well I just can't! Not if you're going to say Matisse!

(They ALL think some more.)

EINSTEIN. How about Rubens?

PICASSO. Oh please.

SAGOT. How about Michelangelo Buonarotti?

GASTON. We haven't got time for everyone to say Nicholangleo Canelloni!

PICASSO. El Greco! We can say El Greco.

GERMAINE. El Greco doesn't make our mouths go in a smile, it makes it go in an "oh". We'll all look like fish.

(In unison, they try "El Grec-oh." They don't like it. They ALL think some more.)

COUNTESS. I've got one, how about "twice"?

(As COUNTESS says it she smiles.)

PICASSO. No! Not "twice".
COUNTESS. Perky?

(Everyone shakes his head "no". They ALL start to think again.)

SCHMENDIMAN. How about "cheese"?

(This stops them. They like it.)

SAGOT. Cheese is good.
SCHMENDIMAN. Chalk up another one for me!
SAGOT. Okay everybody, say "cheese".

(They all say "cheese" and the photo is taken. They are all blinded by the flash.)

SAGOT. Did the flash go off?
SINGER. *(He drinks the vodka and tomato juice.)* A-well-a bless-a-my soul-A what's-a wrong with me? Whew, that's strong stuff. *(Pause as the SINGER looks at the painting.)* Boy oh boy, what a weird paintin'.
GASTON. Weird? It's just sheep.
SINGER. Sheep? Looks like five women to me.

(PICASSO'S head snaps around to the picture.)

SINGER. You puttin' me on? You see sheep?

GASTON. I see sheep, she sees sheep. Everyone in here sees sheep except for you.

SINGER. Well, mercy. It looks like five weird women to me.

PICASSO. *(Stopped.)* Where did you say you were from?

SINGER. From the future.

PICASSO. And why are you here?

SINGER. She sent me with a message.

PICASSO. Who is *she*?

SINGER. She is the one who whispers in your ear every time you touch the pencil to the paper.

PICASSO. And what is the message?

SINGER. Are you open to receive it?

PICASSO. Yes.

SINGER. You better stand back.

PICASSO stands, thinks, then steps back. The SINGER gestures toward the painting. Effect: The painting changes into the full size eight foot square painting of Picasso's "Les Demoiselles D'Avignon". PICASSO and the SINGER stare at the painting in wonder. No one else, of course, sees it. PICASSO turns away from the painting, entranced.)

PICASSO. *(To himself.)* I could dream it forever and still not do it, but when the time comes for it to be done, God I want to be ready for it, to be ready for the moment of convergence between the thing done and the doing of it, between the thing to be made and its maker. At that moment I am speaking for everyone; I am dreaming for the billions yet to come, I am taking the part of us that cannot be understood by God and letting it bleed from the wrist onto the canvas... And it can only be made because I have felt these things: my lust, my greed, my hatred, my happiness. *(Turns to the bar.)* So this is what it's like.

GERMAINE. What?

PICASSO. To be there at the moment.

GASTON. What moment?

PICASSO. The moment I leave blue behind. I'd like some wine.

GERMAINE. Any special color?

PICASSO. *(He looks at the painting.)* Rosé. *(To the SINGER.)* My name is Picasso. Are you an artist?

SINGER. I had my moment.

PICASSO. What kind of moment?

SINGER. I had my moment of... perfection.

PICASSO. I know the feeling. I just had it over there.

SINGER. It's a good feeling.

PICASSO. Yes it is.

SINGER. I think not many people have it.

PICASSO. No, no they don't.

SINGER. Hard to know when it's happening, till it's over.

PICASSO. Don't tell anyone that; better to let them think you always knew.

SINGER. Yes sir.

PICASSO. Don't let anyone in on the fact that we can't help it. We're like the chickens that cross the road. We do it and we don't know why.

SINGER. Yes sir.

PICASSO. And remember, in a sense, we are both exalted, because we are originals.

SINGER. Well, that's a pretty bold statement, Mr. Picasso, considering we both took ideas from the art of the Negro.

(Magic music. The set pulls away, revealing a backdrop of stars in the sky. The painting is still visible. EINSTEIN pops out of his chair, looking up.)

EINSTEIN. Did you see that?

SINGER. The roof is gone.

EINSTEIN. The stars have come out.

PICASSO. Millions and millions of stars.

EINSTEIN. You're way low.

SINGER. It's night. I didn't know it was night, you know, the time traveling thing. I arrive, I don't know if it's lunch or dinner or what. I've put on 18 pounds. Hoping to take it off when I go back.

EINSTEIN. I'm going to get a new suit. When I present my paper, I'd like to be wearing a new suit.

PICASSO. I wonder what I'll be wearing when I paint it?

SINGER. I'd like something white with a big belt. *(Then.)* Did you see that?

EINSTEIN. Shooting star. They hit the atmosphere and burn white.

PICASSO. I'd like to leave a long trail. A long string of fire.

EINSTEIN. From horizon to horizon.

SINGER. Whoosh!

PICASSO. So bright that when you look away, you can still see it against your eyes.

EINSTEIN. I would like that... a retention of vision.

PICASSO. I would like that too. Into my eighties. A retention of vision.

SINGER. I would like to have it too although I don't know what you're talking about.

PICASSO. I hope I don't die young.

EINSTEIN. Me too.

SINGER. *(Gulps.)*

PICASSO. Are you dead?

SINGER. Pretty much.

EINSTEIN. How is it?

SINGER. Overrated.

PICASSO. All those stars. It's a miracle.

EINSTEIN. No, not a miracle; that's just the way it is. A miracle would be if, for example, the stars rearranged themselves and spelled out our names across the heavens.

(They ALL watch agog.)

PICASSO. My God!

EINSTEIN. It's a miracle...

SINGER. Just like Vegas.

PICASSO. There's my name.

EINSTEIN. There's mine; spelled right too.

PICASSO. *(To the SINGER.)* Don't see yours though.

SINGER. Oh yeah, it's there. Right above both of yours and three times as big.

PICASSO/EINSTEIN. Oh yeah.

EINSTEIN. Humph.

SINGER. Get used to it gentlemen, 'cause that's the way it works.

(Pause.)

PICASSO. I want to have the time to make enough things.

EINSTEIN. That's what we do best, make things.

PICASSO. I want to leave the world littered with beauty.

EINSTEIN. I want to make Newton's apple leap back into the tree.

SINGER. I want to come at them through the radio and break their hearts.

PICASSO. I want them to see the thousand years of tenderness in a woman combing her hair.

EINSTEIN. I want an idea to take them at light speed to the edge of the universe.

SINGER. I want them not to be lonesome tonight.

PICASSO. Hey, I think we should toast.

EINSTEIN. Got one?

PICASSO. Got a good one.

SINGER. Sure.

SAGOT. Let's.

FREDDY. I'll pour.

GASTON. I'll drink.

(GERMAINE pours several drinks, distributes in silence.)

PICASSO. I want to toast the twentieth century...

GASTON. Why the twentieth century?

SINGER. Heck, ah know why.

FREDDY. Why?

SINGER. 'Cause this century, the accomplishments of artists and scientists outshone the accomplishments of politicians and governments.

(Pause from everyone.)

GASTON. We shall see.

SINGER. You can take that to the bank.

FREDDY. I know what he means.

GASTON. You always know what everybody means. What exactly does he mean, Freddy?

FREDDY. Simple. He means that in the twentieth century, no movement will be as beautiful as the movement of the line across the paper *(Points to PICASSO.)* the note across the staff *(Indicates the SINGER.)* or the idea across the mind *(Indicates EINSTEIN.).*

GERMAINE. *(To PICASSO.)* See what I mean?

FREDDY. I do what I can. I'll start the toast. You all are pretty good rhymers... *(Steps forward, swings his arm like a pendulum.)* The Pendulum Swings To The Left...

(FREDDY signals to the COUNTESS.)

COUNTESS. *(Shrugs.)* ... The Pendulum Swings To The Right.

(COUNTESS hands it over to GASTON.)

GASTON. The past was driven by horses...

(Sounds of agreement from the others.)

EINSTEIN. The future is driven by light.

(They ALL give a responsive "yeah". It falls to SCHMENDIMAN.)

SCHMINDIMAN. Coconuts...

(He can't think of anything. FREDDY steps in.)

FREDDY. The mistakes of the past are over...

(More "yeahs".)

PICASSO. The Modern waits to be met...

(More enthusiasm. SCHMENDIMAN steps forward.)

SCHMENDIMAN. The pelican's a funny...

(Again SCHMENDIMAN can't think of anything. Sits down.)

SAGOT. Say goodbye to the age of indifference...

(They respond with more "here, heres". SAGOT hands it over to the SINGER.)

SINGER. ... and say hello... *(Everybody anticipates.)* ... to the age... *(Everybody yeah!)*... of regret.

(They ALL start to toast enthusiastically, then on "regret" stop short and stare at the SINGER. Momentary deflation. Then,)

PICASSO. To the twentieth century!
EINSTEIN. To the twentieth century!
EVERYBODY. The twentieth century!

(The lights start to dim--or the curtain starts to drop. The SINGER eyes the lights.)

SINGER. Isn't it amazing how the play fit exactly between the time that the lights came up, and the lights went down? (Or: "the curtain went up and the curtain went down.")

END OF PLAY

PROP LIST

ONSTAGE:
Down Right:
Square Table - on brown spike
Match Pad - on SR side on table (check to make sure still
          good)
Black Chair - US on table
Brown Chair - SR side of table

Center:
Long Table - on brown spike
Long Bench - SR on table
Small Brown Bench - DL on table
Small Black Bench - UL on table

Stage Left:
Rectangle Table
Diamond Chair - DR on table
Reddish brown Chair - UL on table

Up Center:
3 Bar Stools - on brown spike

BAR:
Stage Left End: (check photo)
3 Candles
Pile of Blank Coasters - 3 piles (8,12,8) staggered
2 Small Ashtrays
1 Large Ashtray - dampened
3 Glasses w/Matches - set in ashtrays

Stage Left/Underneath Bar:
x-tra Coasters
2 White Bar Towels
Bar Tray
Slop Bucket - in UR end of bar tray
Dust Pan and Broom - on floor

Up Left Behind Bar:
Garbage Can
          (Bottles set SL to SR)
Brown Rosé Bottle - set on shelf, should be filled at least
          halfway
Full Green Red Wine Bottle - set on shelf
Full Clear Rum Bottle - set on shelf
Full Clear Vodka Bottle - set on shelf

Stage Right End: (check photo)
Statue
Cigarettes - filter down in shot glass
Matches - tip up on shot glass
Match Pad - taped down, check to make sure still good
Newspaper
Coffee Cup w/water
Sharpened Pencils in Brown Cup
Ashtray w/sand
Large Red Checked Rag

Stage Right/Underneath:
(set SL to SR)
9 Large Glasses
8 Small Glasses

Artist Book
Red Courbet Book - staggered, on top of Artist book
Ledger - set on top of Courbet book
Pencil - set it ledger
Cigar Box - set on top of Ledger
4 Worn Pieces of Paper - in cigar box
Extra Scratch Pad - set in bottom of cigar box

Up Right Behind Bar:
(set SL to SR)
Full Green Bottle of red wine
Full Clear Bottle of Vodka
Full Clear Square bottle of Rum
Full Green Bottle of Red Wine
Small Pitcher of Tomato Juice/Water - underneath on SL side
            of shelf
Pitcher of Water - underneath of SR side of shelf

Up Center Behind Bar:
Check Sheep Painting set

Up Left:
Three Sketches on wall

**Check spike marks - 2 brown DCR; 1 brown DC; 1 brown
            DCL**
Return offstage flats SR and SL to onstage position
All doors closed
Check doorstop is in correct position
Check running lights are at level
Check bell and pull

PERSONAL PROPS

Stage Right:
Scarf - Gaston
Suzanne's Cloth Purse
Sketch - set in Suzanne's purse
Germaine's Purse w/Tarot Cards
Money - Countess
Matisse - Sagot
Wallet w/money - Sagot
Three Francs - in Sagot wallet
Cup of **Sharpened** Pencils w/two smaller pencils in it
Einstein's Pipe
Einstein's Tobacco Pouch filled w/tobacco
Small Book - Einstein
Tissues
Cups
Water

Cigars - set on wig shelf
Matches - set on wig shelf
Lighter - set on wig shelf
Ashtray w/sand - set on wig shelf
Camera - set in corner, legs together, **bolt tightened**

Stage Left: (check photo)
Small Red Checked Bar Towel - set on prop shelf
Glitter - set on prop shelf
Coffee Pot - set on prop table
Bottle - set on prop table
Tissues - set on prop table

Cups - set on prop table
Water - set on prop table
Garbage Can - set underneath prop table
Small Bench - set by railing

COSTUME PLOT

PICASSO:
  Black Boots
  Gray/Black pants
  Tan Collarless Striped Shirt
  Interesting Suspenders
  Rust/Orange Scarf
  Green/Black Corduroy Jacket

EINSTEIN:
  Black Boots
  3 Piece Mustard & Black Herringbone Suit
  White Tab Collar Shirt
  Narrow Brown Tie

FREDDY:
  Brown Boots
  Green Pants
  Rust Striped Shirt
  Plaid Vest w/Green Back and Bamboo Buttons
  Pocket Watch
  Green Patterned Jacket
  Tweed Cap
  Peach Plaid Tie

GASTON:
  Black Shoes
  Gray Pants

Pink Checked Shirt
Blue Cardigan Sweater Vest
Pink & Gray Jacket w/Blue Flower in Lapel
Pink, Gray, Blue, Paisley Tie/Ascot
Navy Blue Beret

SAGOT:
Black Oxfords
Mauve Pants
Lavender Vest
Tux Shirt w/High Collar
Lavender Jacket w/Lapel Pin
Gray Gloves
Gray Homburg Hat
Gold Lorgnette on Chain
Ice Blue Ascot Pin
Purple, Silver, Black Ascot

SCHMENDIMAN:
Brown Boots
Tan/Brown Knee Socks
Gold/Green/Brown Plaid Knickers
Gold/Green/Brown Norfolk Jacket
Gold Leather Gloves in jacket pocket
Gold Vest w/Green Buttons
White Shirt
Brown Bowler Hat
Green Bow Tie

ELVIS:
  Blue Suede Shoes
  White Socks
  Black Pants
  Black Belt w/Silver Buckle
  Black Shirt
  Blue/Gray Jacket w/Silver Collar
  Silver Ring

GERMAINE:
  Black Lace-Up Boots
  Black Thigh High Stockings
  2 Petticoats
 Butt pad
  Corset
  Green/Black Floral Skirt
  Green Blouse
  Green/Black Floral Bolero Jacket
  Beaded Purse
  Green/Black/Gray Hat w/Feathers and Net Tie
  Black Beaded Necklace
  Ruby/Green/Black Earrings
  Silver Bracelets

SUZANNE:
  Black Lace-Up Boots
  Black and Gray Striped Stockings
  2 Petticoats

Butt Pad
Corset
Net Tank Top w/Built In Bra
Red Neck Tie
Mauve Blouse
Red/Black Paisley Skirt
Black Velvet Vest
Tapestry Purse
Net Fingerless Gloves
Black Boater Hat w/Plaid Ribbon
Tortoise Shell Hair Comb

COUNTESS:
Black Velvet Dress
Pearl/Emerald Jewel Choker
Black Velvet Gloves
Black Feather Boa
Smokey Glasses
Feathered Hat
Short Petticoat

FEMALE ADMIRER:
Tan/White checked Dress
Mustard Hershey Kiss Hat

THE OFFICE PLAYS
Two full length plays by Adam Bock

THE RECEPTIONIST
Comedy / 2m., 2f. Interior
At the start of a typical day in the Northeast Office, Beverly deals effortlessly with ringing phones and her colleague's romantic troubles. But the appearance of a charming rep from the Central Office disrupts the friendly routine. And as the true nature of the company's business becomes apparent, The Receptionist raises disquieting, provocative questions about the consequences of complicity with evil.

"...Mr. Bock's poisoned Post-it note of a play."
- New York Times

"Bock's intense initial focus on the routine goes to the heart of
The Receptionist's pointed, painfully timely allegory... elliptical,
provocative play..."
- Time Out New York

THE THUGS
Comedy / 2m, 6f / Interior
The Obie Award winning dark comedy about work, thunder and the mysterious things that are happening on the 9th floor of a big law firm. When a group of temps try to discover the secrets that lurk in the hidden crevices of their workplace, they realize they would rather believe in gossip and rumors than face dangerous realities.

"Bock starts you off giggling, but leaves you with a chill."
- Time Out New York

"... a delightfully paranoid little nightmare that is both more
chillingly realistic and pointedly absurd than anything
John Grisham ever dreamed up."
- New York Times

CPSIA information can be obtained at www.ICGtesting.com
Printed in the USA
LVOW01s1117110815

449650LV00013B/119/P